THE HERON

AND OTHER

FABLES

THE HERON

AND OTHER

FABLES

DON GRIFFIN

ISBN: 978-0-9865552-2-0
Photos by Don Griffin

Also by Don Griffin:
Einstein Didn't Say That (2010)
ISBN: 978-0-9865552-0

To Olga

INTRODUCTION

For years I operated a food truck. I drove from factory to factory cooking for the workers.

This never felt like work. In fact it felt like an escape from work. The people I served were the ones doing the real work of making real things.

After a hectic lunch hour I might postpone dealing with the heat and mess of my mobile kitchen and seek cool refuge in the library.

Sometimes I would read, and sometimes I would just take out a notebook and write down the words "Once there was..."on it, and wait for a thought to come.

Over time a couple of notebooks were filled with what I called 'my stupid little stories'.

So here they are, all packed up and stuffed unwillingly into categories. If any of them should manage to entice a smile or a nod from a reader or two I will be happy.

TABLE OF CONTENTS

PART ONE: MONEY

PART TWO: WORK

PART THREE: DEBT

PART FOUR: WEALTH

PART FIVE: CHANGE

PART SIX: INTENTION

PART SEVEN: WONDER

part one

money

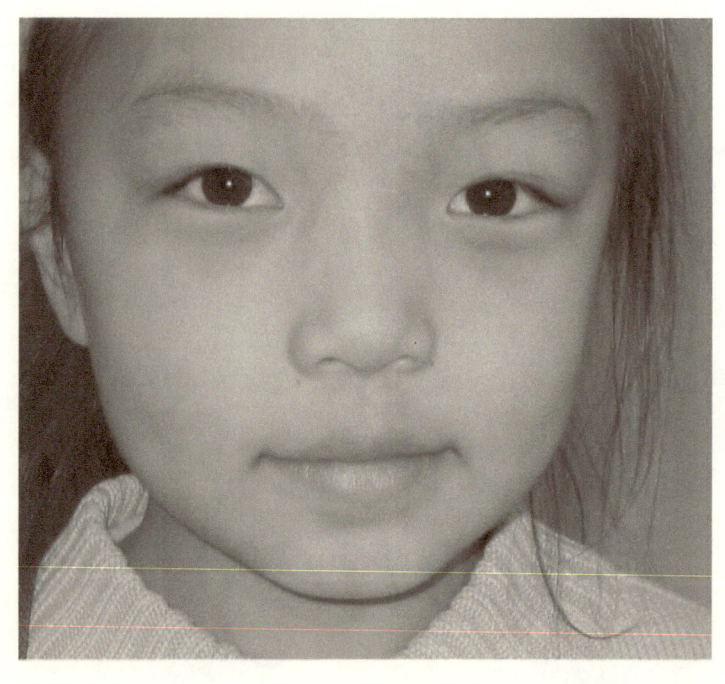

THE QUESTION

Once there was an economics professor who was visiting the classroom of his young daughter. Like the other parents in the room he had come to talk to the children about his job.

When his turn came he showed them some cash from his pocket and asked if they knew what it was.

When they had identified each piece of currency he asked them to think about the whole idea of money.

He explained that the bills and coins themselves had little worth. They were just guarantees that you could get things. They were in fact small promises.

Just as the professor was feeling good about helping the children understand, his daughter's best friend asked:

"When prices change, do the promises break?"

THE STICKS

Once there was a group of young children who decided that it would be fun to create their own money. They didn't want to copy the paper or metal money that their parents used; their money had to be unique.

They had a clubhouse which was made of old boards that they had found near a house that was under construction. Each day on their way to the clubhouse the children liked to walk through the new house and see what the carpenters had done that day.

One day they found a pile of small lumber cuttings that were being thrown out, and someone suggested that they could make their money out of these sticks. And so they collected all that they could carry and took them to the clubhouse.

In order to be able to tell which sticks would count as money, each child made a special mark on each one. Now only the properly marked sticks would count as money. When they had marked enough sticks they divided them evenly among themselves.

Wanting to try out the new money they practiced using it to trade things with each other. They had to promise that the trades would be real. Otherwise their money would not be real, and that would take all the fun out of it.

A few weeks later one boy's mother noticed him going out on a cold day without his shoes. Calling for him to wait, she went to his bedroom to get them for him.

When she opened the door she found the room completely empty except for a pile of strangely marked sticks.

THE VISITOR

Once there was a beautiful little kingdom on an isolated island. Food was plentiful and the people were physically active as well as creative. The people were always finding new things to do and creating new things to share with each other.

One day a visitor came from a far away land. All the people were curious about the visitor's possessions, especially those shiny little things that were called 'money'.

The visitor explained how the coins were used and the people played endlessly with them, trading them back and forth for this and that.

The king was especially interested when he learned that upon each coin was imprinted the face of a king. He ordered that some be made with his own face on them.

Gradually the people became accustomed to using the coins when they shared things. Gradually the people began to value things that they had not cared about before, according to how many coins someone else had paid for them. Gradually the people began to value the coins themselves.

And now they spent less time finding new things to do, or creating new things to share with each other.

Some of the people in the kingdom wondered if things would change back again, when the visitor went home.

THE DEPOSIT

Once there was a large family traveling together on the desert. They earned their livelihood by selling to people in one community items which they had bought in another.

Back and forth they moved across the sands, buying selling and trading. They needed to carry many different kinds of currency, and it was complicated trying to keep up to date with the fluctuating values of all of them.

Eventually the family decided to print its own currency for use among its members. They had a large number of coins made which were engraved with gorgeous and meaningful images.

The problem was that the beautiful coins were very heavy to carry, and so it was decided that some of them would be deposited in a certain bank for safekeeping when the family travelled long distances.

After a particularly long journey the family returned to the bank to pick up their coins. But they learned that due to much admiration of the coins by the local population, their coins had doubled in value.

Of course this meant that the family could retrieve only half of the coins they had deposited.

THE PEACHES

Once there was a woman who sold peaches in the market in the town where she lived. She had been doing this for so long that she was known affectionately as the 'peach lady'. People were very fond of her and bought peaches from her at the market every week.

One day a local farm boy came to the market to sell the first crop of peaches from a grove of trees that his father had planted years earlier. The boy's peaches were bigger, juicier, more colourful and cheaper than the ones that the peach lady was selling.

That day there were twice as many peaches at the market but almost none were sold.

People did not want to be disloyal to the peach lady, but neither did they want to buy an inferior, more expensive product.

THE WEDDING CAR

Once there was a young girl who was chosen to make paper flowers to decorate her big sister's wedding car.

The girl was very excited about the task, and she wanted to make as many flowers as possible. She decided to ask some of her friends to help.

When a couple of the friends asked how much they would be paid for their work, the girl was bewildered.

She told them that if her sister had wanted 'bought' flowers, she would have gone to the store.

TIME

A small girl asked her father: "What could I buy with all the money in the world?"

Her father answered: "I didn't study economics. Ask your mother."

Her mother answered: "I didn't study sociology. Ask you grandfather."

Her grandfather answered: "I didn't study politics or even psychology for that matter. Ask your grandmother"

Her grandmother answered: "Yes, I studied all of those things, and they all play a part."

Then she continued:

"That's why I think that if you had all the money in the world you could buy everything that was for sale, but only if you could buy it all at exactly the same time."

part two

work

THE MEASUREMENT

Once there was a young fellow who decided to measure the value of all of the work done in his country, including the true value of all the unpaid work being done in peoples' homes.

This would give the government and the citizens a better understanding of their economy and help them appreciate the true value of all the unpaid work that was being done every day.

His work was much discussed by the public and he received high praise from government. However, when he went home he found his house in disarray and his family dejected.

His family complained that they could not engage in any activity upon which he would not be tempted to impose a price. They could not play with the dog without wondering if it was worth more than washing the dishes.

The man went into his study and spent several hours reviewing and organizing his files. He then took them carefully in his car down to the park by the river, where he placed them gently in a barrel and set them on fire.

THE GARDEN

Once there was a large garden shared by five neighbours. From the garden they took enough food to feed their families, and what was left they sold to a market vendor.

Side by side they worked each day and in the evenings they talked while their children played together. Often as they talked they were thinking of ways to make the garden more profitable.

Finally one day they decided that one of them should buy the shares of the other four, and run the garden like a business. The idea was that with one person in control following a clear plan, efficiency would result.

Efficiency did indeed result. The new owner quickly learned that the most profit could be made by growing a single high value cash crop. First he mortgaged the garden and used the money to buy specialized equipment. Then he hired one of his friends to operate the equipment and another one to take care of sales and management.

Finding their new jobs challenging and the wages good, these friends became very dedicated. They worked much longer hours than they had before but visited each other less frequently.

Before long the owner found it unnecessary to be at the garden very much and moved to a large new house several miles away.

The fourth friend took a job in the city working for the company which handled the mortgage and insurance for the garden, and bought a condominium downtown.

The fifth neighbour stayed in his old farmhouse but had no land and no work. He saw his old friends only on special occasions, and when they stopped by with gifts.

All of the friends missed their evening conversations, the sounds of their children playing together, and the taste of freshly picked vegetables.

THE GROCERY CLERK

Once there was a man who worked in a grocery store. Each morning he carefully checked the items on display to be sure that they were still fresh enough to sell. He threw away anything that he would not have been willing to buy or to eat himself.

This involved more expertise and experience than most people realized. One could not always determine freshness by appearance alone. He felt very good knowing that his customers depended on his judgment.

One day the man's nephew, who was making a film for a school project, asked if the man would be willing to act in the film and he agreed to do it as a favor. He played the part of a man who worked in a grocery store.

The film turned out so well that it was shown in theaters and the man was kept busy for quite a while discussing his acting experience in interviews with the media.

The more questions that were asked of the man the more he tried to satisfy the interviewers and the audiences by thinking of more things to say about the film. By paying attention to peoples' reactions he became better at knowing what to say.

This was not at all like working in the grocery store, and the man felt his personality changing. Now, instead of using his own judgment to choose the best things for his customers, he depended on the judgment of the audience members to tell him what to think.

Everyone had a different opinion and soon nothing made sense to him. Despondent and confused, the man told his nephew he did not want to act in any more movies.

It was good that the clerk returned to his old job when he did, since there were many items on the shelves which were long past their best.

No one else in the store had the courage to trust their own judgment about what to keep and what to throw out.

THE ACTOR

Once there was a young film actor whose uncle worked in a grocery store. The young man loved acting because it was an opportunity to express himself honestly and without reservation. He also enjoyed explaining to interviewers and audiences the methods which helped him keep his film roles real and meaningful.

One day when the uncle knew that his nephew was not busy filming, he called to ask him if he wouldn't mind helping out at the store just for a little while, and the nephew agreed to do it as a favor.

The store customers liked the young actor very much and some had seen his films. Business improved as more customers came in to meet and chat with the actor.

Because of this the nephew stayed at the store longer than originally planned. Customers got used to him being there and began to feel comfortable coming to him with minor complaints.

Some would say that the fruit was too hard while others thought it was too soft. Some thought the vegetables needed to be sprayed with water and others complained that this just made them heavier and more expensive.

The nephew learned what to say to satisfy the customers but felt as if his personality was changing. Now instead of explaining how he felt about things, he could only react to how the customers felt.

Despondent and confused, the man told his uncle that he couldn't work at the grocery store any more.

THE NEW MANAGER

Once there was a woman who worked in a clothing factory. The wages were poor and the work was tedious. In order to relieve her boredom she would challenge herself by trying to work faster and faster. But the other workers became angry because it made them look slow.

And so the woman developed a new challenge for herself. Whenever she finished a garment too quickly she would embroider a small design of her own creation in an inconspicuous corner where it would not be noticeable.

This went on for a long time without being noticed by management. However, in the stores where the clothes were being sold the embroidery was indeed being noticed. Customers were seeking out the items with the hand-sewn designs, and salespeople were charging a premium for them.

When the factory owners discovered this they did several things. They raised their prices. Then they encouraged all the employees to learn how to embroider. And finally, they promoted the woman who had started it all.

In her new position as general manager the first change she introduced was profit sharing for all of the workers.

As a result the workers began challenging themselves to find new ways to get the work done faster.

Gradually they noticed their wages improving and the work becoming less tedious.

THE SALE

Once there was a business in which all of the workers belonged to a union. One day the owner of the business met with the union members and told them that if the business was to remain competitive their wages would have to be lowered.

Afterwards the union members gathered again to discuss the possibility of going on strike. The problem was that if the owner was correct they could end up losing their jobs altogether. They trusted the owner and believed he was telling them the truth.

They debated for many long hours. They could not agree on a pay reduction. Surprisingly the only thing they could agree on was that they trusted the owner since he had been good to each of them individually.

They invited the owner to join the discussion and soon he came up with a plan. Rather than see his business decline or have his workers lose their jobs he offered them a deal.

In exchange for their participation in his plan he would divide the ownership of the business evenly among everyone and keep an equal share for himself.

For the next few months they all worked harder than ever for wages lower than any competitor was paying, and the former owner did his share of the work.

Soon they had tripled the business and profits exploded. Within a short time investors were coming from far and wide to see this astonishingly profitable business. They all wanted to buy shares.

When this excitement about their business reached its peak, the owner-workers sold their shares for more money than they would have earned for years of work at the union rate of pay.

Then they said their goodbyes to each other, and set off to find something else to do.

THE BAKER

One day a baker's assistant was sitting on an upturned bucket behind the shop, drinking his coffee. He didn't use the lunchroom because he liked to sit by the open back door and smell the bread baking.

There were a hundred things he could tell about the bread in the ovens, just from the smell. The temperature, the ingredients, the strength of the yeast and dozens of other subtleties came in and out of his attention as he thought of other problems.

He was thinking of all the bills he had to pay and wondering if his paycheck would cover them. This led him to think about how clever those people must be who made a lot of money.

The more he thought about it the more he thought he must be stupid. To prove himself wrong, he went back to school. He borrowed money and got government grants and completed an advanced degree in food science.

Soon he found himself in charge of a research laboratory earning three times his old salary. His responsibility was to test newly developed types of grain flour and new bread-baking equipment.

He was much respected by his colleagues for his great knowledge, but they wondered why he always took his coffee outside the back door instead of joining them in the lunchroom.

part three

debt

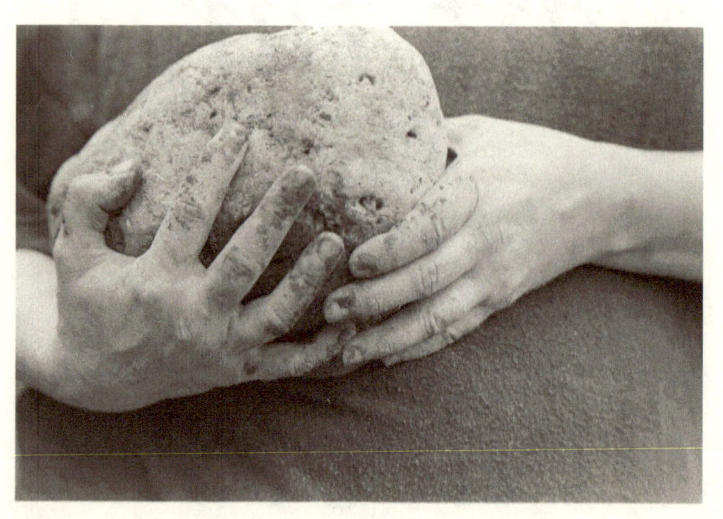

THE MOUNTAIN

Once there was a woman who spent her time carrying rocks from one side of a mountain to the other. When she had made a very large pile she would begin carrying them back again, one by one.

When people from the nearby town asked her why she did this she would say that she was building a city.

Since she was not being paid for this strange effort people came to believe that she must have been both independently wealthy and a little bit crazy.

Now it happened that the town came upon hard times. There was unemployment and poverty. Little was being produced because little was being sold. People were getting ready to leave the town to look for work.

Then one day there appeared a notice in the town newspaper saying that many helpers were needed to work on the mountain. When people arrived they discovered that the crazy rich woman was hiring people to carry her rocks. She had half of them carrying the rocks one way and the other half carrying them back the other way. No sooner was a rock put down on one side of the mountain than it was picked up and carried back to the other side.

Saying that she was too busy supervising the work to go to the bank for money, the woman paid the workers with a signed handwritten note for each day's work. Merchants in town, believing as everyone did that the woman was rich and crazy, gave the workers goods in return for these notes. Before long the notes came to be accepted as readily as cash.

Now that the people could make purchases, everything changed. Businesses thrived. More people were needed to work in the stores and factories. New homes and roads needed to be built. And so one by one the rock carriers returned to work in the growing town and before long the town had become a city.

Eventually the woman was alone again on the mountain, carrying her rocks from one side to the other. When people asked her why she did this she said that it helped her think and kept her strong.

THE BIKER

Once there was a man who borrowed some money from a lending company to buy a motorcycle.

Because he was able to make only small payments on the loan it was going to take him a long time to pay it back.

Most of the money he paid took care of the interest only, and not the loan itself. It seemed to him that he would never be out of debt.

Then one day he went to a second lending company and borrowed enough to pay off the first. The next day he went back to the first company and took out a larger loan and paid off the second loan with interest.

He repeated this process until each company was making large amounts of interest from the huge loans they were giving to the man who had become their biggest and most reliable customer.

Everyone was happy and everyone except the man had forgotten about the motorcycle. Finally one day he borrowed enough money from each business to buy the other one. Then he closed them both down.

He had the sensation that his motorcycle had become lighter and more responsive to his touch.

THE SOCCER BALL

A young boy loaned his little brother enough money to buy a soccer ball. The arrangement was that there would be a small interest charge and a payment made each week.

The older boy was very fair and would even adjust the payments for the weeks when his brother was short of money. The younger boy was very diligent and eventually the loan was paid in full.

By the time the boys grew up they no longer shared the same attitude toward work.

The older man measured the value of his own work by the results it achieved.

The younger brother measured the value of his own work by the amount of time and effort it involved.

THE BICYCLE

Once there was a young woman who worked in the loans department of a small bank. One day when she was visiting her parents' home her younger sister asked her how she might borrow enough money to buy a bicycle.

The older sister said that the bank would not likely be willing but she could lend the money to her sister herself. In order to teach the younger girl respect for money she decided to charge her interest in the same manner as the bank.

As she gave the money to her sister she included a friendly lesson about money. She explained that money should be thought of as a tool and used carefully just as one would use any other tool. The interest would help the young borrower remember to be careful with money.

A few months later she again visited her parents' home. Right away she noticed the shiny yellow bicycle locked to the front garden gate. It was spotlessly clean and obviously well cared for.

As soon as she saw her younger sister she complimented her on taking such good care of the bicycle and asked if she could take it for a ride.

"Of course" replied the young girl, and they walked together toward the locked bicycle. As the proud young owner carefully removed the chain, she pointed out all the unique and advanced features on the beautiful machine.

"There's only one more thing" the girl continued: "How much should I charge you for using my bicycle, so that you will remember to take care of it?"

THE SON

Once there was a man who worked long hours at a rather uninteresting job for a wage so low that his family could barely survive.

Everyone in the community felt badly for the man but they had heard that if his pay were to be increased his employer would lose business to competitors and the man would have no job at all.

And so being too busy and too tired to look for other work the man struggled on. Then one day his oldest son came to work with him after school, just to help his tired father.

The boy worked well and the owner was pleased but explained to the boy that he couldn't afford to pay him. In response the boy asked if he might suggest an idea.

Then he asked the owner to credit him with one-quarter of what his father earned and to hold it for him at a reasonable rate of interest until he graduated.

The owner agreed and the boy worked hard. Production and profits went up and expenses went down. Several years went by and when the boy finally graduated he came to collect his pay.

When the amount owing was calculated and the interest added, the owner was unable to pay. He had to forfeit the business to the boy and his father.

Now the former owner needed a job, so they kindly offered to hire him. But the man declined, explaining that his family could not survive on the company's low wages.

part four

wealth

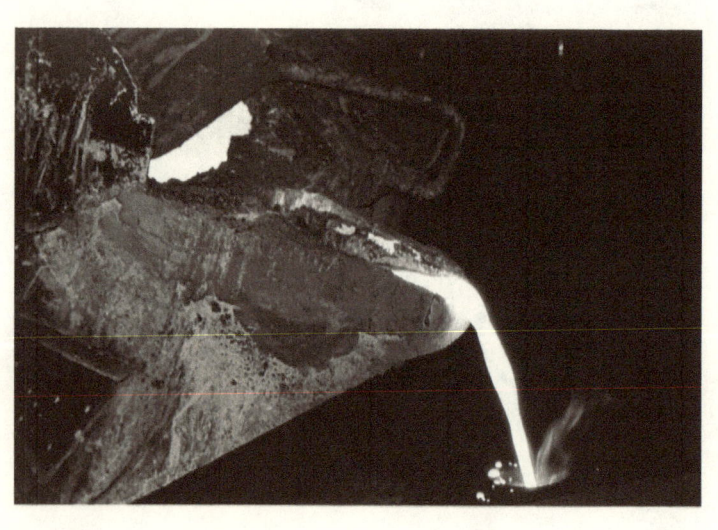

THE THEORIES

Once there was a man who had worked all his life in a foundry pouring hot iron. He happened to turn on his television one evening when a discussion was taking place among expert economists who had gathered to debate the question of how wealth is created.

The economists offered complicated theories and argued brilliantly about which was correct. As he listened, the man was thinking that every day at work it was easy to see wealth being created.

When the experts began repeating themselves he got bored and changed the channel.

THE BIRDHOUSE

Once there was a man who loved business.

Even as a child he had been fascinated by the idea that with a little work and a bit of material he could create something worth more than the value of the work added to the value of the material.

He hoped his own son would share this appreciation.

When the boy sold his first birdhouse, which he had made out of scrap wood, the man said to him: "Good, son. Now pay yourself for the work you did, and whatever money you have left over is newly created wealth."

The boy thought this over before asking his father: "Does that mean that the less I pay myself, the more wealth I have created?"

THE CURIOSITY

Once there was a man who was making his way across a lonely desert to deposit a small amount of cash into a bank.

He reasoned that if he invested the money instead of carrying it around it would increase in value.

He would return one day and take the money out again to buy a beautiful new home for his retirement.

But somewhere in the middle of the desert he was bitten by a magical snake and fell into a deathly sleep.

For a hundred years he lay there buried in the sand.

While he was asleep the town that he had been looking for grew larger and closer until one day a road-builder uncovered him and he awoke.

Dazed and shaken he set off again to find the bank.

But when he got there and put his money down the young clerks looked at him kindly and explained that his old money was worthless.

Only the new type of money had value because it represented a fixed amount of gold.

Confused and dejected, the man turned to walk out of the bank. As he did so a woman who had been in line behind him stepped up and offered to give him some of her new bills in exchange for his old ones.

She said that she was a collector and only wanted his money because it was so rare. It was a curiosity.

This made no more sense to the man than all of the other strange things which had already happened to him. He declined her offer and left the bank.

For days he wandered the streets of the town accepting handouts and trying to understand it all.

In the meantime the news about this strange man and his rare old money began to spread about the town.

The more people heard about him the more they wanted some of that money, just as a curiosity.

The longer he wandered and refused the offers the more new money they offered him, until he finally had to accept a big box of it just to get some peace.

When he finally collected his thoughts, he decided to leave the box of money at the bank before beginning his long walk back across the desert.

When he got to the bank the young clerks smiled kindly at him just as before. After a short conversation with them he decided on a new plan.

Instead of walking back across the desert he would take long walks in the park by the river, and try to learn all about the new ways.

In the evenings he would invite the neighbors to visit with him on the verandah of his beautiful new home.

THE APPLE

Once there was a little girl who found an apple which had fallen from a tree in her neighbour's orchard. This apple was the sweetest, reddest, tastiest-looking apple she had ever seen.

Hungry as she was, she could not bring herself to take a bite and spoil its perfection. She showed it to everyone but would not let them touch.

Some offered to buy it and some suggested she enter it in a competition and some said she should just eat it.

Finally she decided to give the apple to a quiet little boy who had said nothing but only stared in wonder. She told the boy to eat the apple and plant all of its seeds.

THE NEWS

Once there was a woman who wanted to buy a certain house. The price was just barely within her borrowing limits which had been set by the bank.

The manager at the bank had agreed to approve a mortgage for her, but advised her to think carefully before going so deeply into debt.

Taking this advice seriously, she went away for a week to a friend's cabin in the woods. In this place she was completely isolated and could collect her thoughts in peace.

At the end of the week she felt confident that she had properly considered all the pros and cons and risks involved, and she decided to go ahead with the purchase.

When she submitted her offer to buy the house the sales agent told her that the house was still for sale and that she could still be approved for a mortgage and that the monthly payments would probably still be the same as the bank manager had quoted a week earlier.

What had changed was that the number of payments needed to pay for the house had doubled. This was because while she was away the price of the house had also doubled.

Too shocked and dumfounded to feel outrage, the woman went directly to the bank to ask the manager if he knew what was going on.

The manager quickly realized that because she had been away at her friend's cabin for a week, the woman had not heard the news. Someone had discovered a new vitamin which would double everyone's lifespan.

The real estate market had adjusted quickly to the news.

THE FLOWERS

Once there was an old philosopher who had saved a large amount of money.

One day a friend asked her: "How can you be wealthy and study truth? Doesn't your wealth change how you think about the meaning of life?"

The old philosopher had the answer ready: "I used to collect flowers." she replied. "But they required care. Now that I collect money instead, I have a lot more time to study the ultimate beauty which both flowers and money represent."

The friend considered this statement for a moment before responding thoughtfully: "I think you are right about one thing. You will need the extra time."

part five

change

THE HOSPITAL ROOM

One day a woman was driving home from work and became involved in a bad accident.

It happened that the driver of the other car was a woman of about the same age. The two had similar injuries, were taken to the same hospital and even shared the same room for several days.

During this time their lawyers had been discussing who would have to pay for damages and injuries.

In the small hospital room filled with flowers it was difficult to avoid conversation, and despite being cautioned by their lawyers, the women became friends.

By the time they were ready to be dismissed from the hospital, they had agreed upon two things.

The first was that they would visit each other regularly, and the second was that they wouldn't need their lawyers.

They used the money they saved on the lawyers to buy nicer cars, and they used the nice cars for their visits.

THE TIGER

Once on a mountain there lived an old tiger who was revered as the master hunter. In the valley stood a large automotive plant which was revered as the tiger of industry.

The younger tigers on the mountain competed with each other for the attention of the old master because they all wanted to learn from him the secrets of hunting for food.

The smaller workshops in the valley competed with each other to make parts for the automobile factory, and each learned how to make certain parts very efficiently.

The old tiger soon realized he did not have to hunt anymore, since the younger ones were so eager to please him and gave him plenty to eat.

The automobile company gradually stopped all manufacturing and just assembled the parts made by the smaller plants.

Eventually the young tigers on the mountain had learned so much from the old master that they no longer needed him. But since he was now almost toothless they saved the most tender pieces of meat for him.

In time the small companies in the valley learned to make their parts fit together so easily that assembling an automobile had become a simple matter. They began to sell their parts to small workshops which specialized in assembly, and sent nothing to the old factory.

Today the old tiger watches his grandchildren play in the valley where the factory used to be.

THE STONES

Once there was a group of children who found some colourful stones. Their problem was that they could not agree on the fairest way to share them.

The oldest wanted the most. The one who had found the first one felt entitled to a bigger share. The one who had picked up the most wanted to keep them.

The more they argued the more each thought of reasons why he or she should have more.

Just then an old woman happened by. She had lived in the area for a long time and had played there as a child herself.

Quickly she saw the problem and quickly she had a solution. She said to the children:

"If you can divide the stones fairly before I count to ten, I will tell you where there are hundreds more."

THE NEW ORDER

Once there was a man who decided to see how much money he could save for his retirement. He worked at several jobs, lived alone in a small room and ate the meanest of survival meals.

But just as he was about to retire on his fortune a new government was elected. The new government announced that due to an emergency situation it was necessary that all money being kept in private savings accounts would become the property of the state.

Wondering how this terrible situation could have come about the man went out and got a newspaper. It felt odd to be spending money on something that he would not keep and could not eat.

On page three of the newspaper he found a scholarly article summarizing the factors which had led to such an unexpected election result and such a drastic announcement.

According to the article there had been so many people hoarding their money during the last three decades that many businesses had closed due to slow sales.

With so many people spending so little money a large percentage of the population had become unemployed.

The article showed a graph which described the point at which this group of unemployed became large enough to determine the outcome of the election.

By popular vote it had been decided that private savings should be used to support the unemployed.

THE PUBLIC SPEAKER

Once in a small village there lived a man who saw that the rules everyone lived by favoured the rich. And so he began to speak out in public about this unfairness.

There should be more and better rules.

It was so easy to see that he was right that people became angry, and before too long he found himself elected to a position of power.

With this power he set about making more and more rules, but each time he made a new rule somebody would find a way to use it to gain an unfair advantage.

Eventually he resigned his position and went back to speaking in public.

This time he did not give lectures which made everyone angry. Instead he asked people questions which made them think.

It soon became unnecessary to have so many rules.

THE FORMULA

Once there was a great teacher to whom people regularly came for advice. He was by reputation a very spiritual person but his answers to problems tended to be quite practical.

One day some council members from a nearby town came to him with an economic problem. All of the number scales which were supposed to measure the economic health of the town were very positive.

The charts were rising where they should rise and falling where they were supposed to fall. The banks had plenty of money and everyone was busy.

The problem was that there was a great disparity between the earnings of people in various occupations.

Although everyone worked hard some were getting rich and some were falling into poverty.

The townspeople wanted to find a way of resolving this inequality. What they did not want was to infringe upon free market forces or to discourage ambition or inventiveness.

After the great teacher had heard all that the townspeople wanted to tell him, he replied that he knew of a secret mathematical formula which he alone could use to solve their problem.

In order for him to use this formula huge amounts of data would be needed.

The teacher instructed the council members to go back

to their town and ask all of the people to write their names and their weekly incomes on a list which the council members would then post in the town square.

On the same list right beside the income amount was a space in which each person was required to indicate whether they thought their own income was too low, too high or just right.

This exercise was to be performed each week and the town's accountants were to sort, total and make graphs of all of this information and give it to the councillors, who would then bring it to the teacher.

Many weeks went by and for many weeks the teacher would say only that he needed more data and reminded the councillors that the formula was very complicated.

The more time that went by and the more data they gave to the teacher the less they believed that there would ever be an answer. Some even doubted that the teacher had a secret formula at all.

Gradually they became less regular about bringing the data to the teacher. Some of the councillors stopped making the trip to see him.

Also the townspeople themselves had become less conscientious about adding their data to the list. It was odd that as the weeks went by fewer and fewer people seemed to care about the teacher's formula.

It was also odd that with each week there was less and less disparity in the incomes of the people in the town.

THE KINGDOM

Once there was a powerful king who had two infant sons. When the boys were just over one year old the king began to consider how he might ensure that they grew up to be as strong as himself.

He feared that a life of luxury might make them weak. Furthermore if they lived in the palace they would not be challenged by others of their own age in competitions of strength and skill.

The king therefore decided on a plan which would make them compete not only with others but with each other.

The king arranged for the boys to be separated and raised by two different families as their own children. The boys were not to be told of their true identity.

When the boys were grown to manhood and had finished all their schooling the king announced a competition. He would on that day give a certain amount of money to every person their age.

Whichever of these people had the most money at the end of a ten year period would inherit his entire kingdom.

As it turned out one of his sons quickly turned his share of the money into a large fortune through hard work and cooperating with others to explore new opportunities.

On the appointed day the king transferred his kingdom to this son. After he had done so he called for the other son to come forward and he told them both for the first time that they were brothers and that he was their real father. The new young king was so shocked by this revelation that he could not speak for three days.

He knew that everyone expected him to give special treatment and large amounts of property to his brother.

But he could not escape the feeling that nothing had really changed, and that no real relationships had been created by the new knowledge.

He wanted to give special treatment to his brother but he could not accept that his brother had suddenly become more deserving than all the others in the kingdom.

In the end the new king kept what he had earned for himself, and divided the rest of the kingdom equally among all the people, including his brother and both of his fathers.

THE MAILBOX

Once there was a pair of birds who were building a nest in an old abandoned mailbox.

They flew here and there and walked about looking at this and that, collecting the best leaves and twigs and whatever odd bits of material that looked useful.

Then one of them happened to find just the most perfect little branch she had ever seen. It was a gem. Soft dry leaves hung gently from the smooth-barked slender and supple stem.

She called to her mate and showed him this perfect item. Together they gently and carefully carried it to the mailbox but alas it was too long. It would not fit inside.

For a long time they carried it about looking for another place to build or another way to make it fit but without success.

The more they tried and failed the more determined they became not to give up on their branch. Incredibly perfect, it represented all that they dreamed of in the life they were building together.

But now they would have to either forget about the branch or abandon the territory that they had staked out.

Unable to decide what to do they left the branch half way in and half way out of the mailbox, knowing how silly it must look and how it broke all the rules of building.

And as time went by they fell into the habit of landing on the sticking-out part when they came home, and would even sit on it together sometimes in the evening.

It was on one such evening that the first of many neighbours came by to ask for advice about how one might build such a wonderful nest.

part six

intention

THE OWNERS

Once there was a young student who took a summer job on a construction site carrying supplies to carpenters and bricklayers who were building an apartment complex.

The weather was hot and the days were long and the breaks were short. At lunchtime it was her habit to sit under a certain tree where there was some shade and eat her sandwiches.

In this spot she could relax and contemplate the progress being made on the building. She also became interested in a colony of ants who were building a large anthill near her tree. They never seemed to rest.

As the weeks went on and both projects were nearing completion she began to wonder if the ants who were building the hill would be the same ants who would live in it, or whether they were just builders like her own crew.

She also wondered whether the ants who lived in the hill would be the ones who owned it, or whether there were special owner ants.

And, if there were special owner ants, did they dream of one day owning more and more anthills?

It was while she was contemplating this last question that she remembered that the paving crew was scheduled to arrive the following week.

The question of ownership became less important.

THE EXECUTIVE

Once there was a woman who had no children of her own but took a caring interest in the children of her neighbours. The family next door had a very earnest and motivated young son who was interested in everything.

The neighbour woman spent a lot of time helping the boy with his schoolwork. She taught him how to focus on achieving the goals set for him by his teachers and eventually he graduated from a respected university with a degree in business.

Before long the young man was hired by a large corporation and earned several promotions very quickly. Success came easily as he continued to focus on the goals set out for him.

When he was finally appointed president of the company his new goal was explained very simply to him by the board of directors. His goal was to make a profit for the shareholders. Under his leadership the company's profits grew and the shareholders were very happy.

One day when he was visiting his parents the man noticed the woman next door tending her garden. He went outside and called to her, wanting to share the story of his success and thank her once again for her teaching.

The woman waited for him to get very close. She took his hand and looked sadly into his eyes. "You must forgive me." she said, "I am so ashamed. I have been watching your career in the news and I have seen you put profits before all else. I am so sorry. I was a very bad teacher. I taught you to let other people set goals for you, and now you have forgotten how to think for yourself."

THE FRUGAL MAYOR

Once there was a town which was having economic troubles. More money was being spent and less work was getting done. When election time came a new mayor was chosen who promised to cut costs in the public sector.

The first thing the new mayor did was to privatize services such as garbage collecting. The reasoning was that having private companies compete for the work would reduce operating costs, and money would be saved.

As a result of these changes many of the people who had been collecting garbage for the town now did the same work for the private companies at lower wages. The same amount of work was being done for less money, just as the mayor had predicted.

The workers now had less money to spend and so they bought fewer products. As a result fewer workers were needed in other industries.

This increase in the number of unemployed in the private sector meant that more government workers were needed to administer social services.

Some of the people who had been collecting garbage were trained for social work and earned good salaries.

Eventually so many social service workers were needed that the town could no longer afford garbage collection.

THE PERCENTAGE

Once there was a very fair-minded governor of a small country. Fairness and equality were of utmost importance to her. Seeing that there was growing disparity of income among her citizens, she decided to make some rules about payment for various types of work, and solve the problem once and for all.

She had a panel of advisers establish a fair level of pay for each job in the country. When the panel had finished this important task, the governor declared that in keeping with the principles of fairness and equality, everyone would get the same percentage increase in pay at exactly the same time every year.

Amazingly, no one had taken the time to realize that by applying the same percentage to everyone, higher earners got bigger increases. The disparity in the yearly increases increased exponentially as years passed.

As a result some people saw things getting better, and some worse. As usual, everyone donated as much as they could afford to give, to various political campaigns.

Naturally, those who were doing better could afford to donate more, and so with each election the governor received more and more campaign donations from those who had benefited from her policies.

She spent the money on messages about fairness and equality, and kept getting re-elected.

When income disparity became worse than it had ever been previously, she was replaced by someone else who also had very good intentions.

THE TRADITIONS

Once there were two wandering tribes who lived on opposite sides of a huge desert. In the middle of the desert was a large rocky basin which collected water when the rainy season came.

The people of one of the tribes believed that in order to show respect to the rain gods they must wait for the basin to become full before drinking any of the water.

The other tribe believed that it would be disrespectful to the rain gods not to drink the rainwater as soon as it fell or even as it was falling.

Both tribes believed that the members of the other tribe were immoral savages who would be punished in due course by the rain gods.

THE TWINS

Once there was a woman who loved music.

She wished that she had studied piano longer as a child, and wanted to make sure that her twin daughters practiced regularly.

It happened that one of the girls loved practicing while the other hated it. The woman thought hard about how she could make the second child enjoy the effort more.

Finally she decided to pay the girl for the time she spent practicing, just as if it were a regular part-time job. Of course to be fair she paid the other child also.

At first both girls practiced and both girls progressed and their mother was pleased.

Eventually the girl who had hated to play began to appreciate the music and played for her own enjoyment.

The girl who had loved to practice gave up on the piano altogether. She found a regular part-time job which paid more than she had been earning from her mother.

THE PERFORMANCE

Once there was a traveling entertainer who performed a one-man show night after night in cities and towns across the land.

The business arrangements and scheduling were all taken care of by his manager, so he never had to think about how much he was being paid and could concentrate on his act.

One night a woman came backstage after the show and told him that while she had long been a fan, this was by far the best performance she had seen the man give.

After thanking her the entertainer sat wondering about this evaluation, since he thought that the show had gone rather badly.

The next day he received many more such compliments from everyone he met.

He also received an engraved plaque thanking him for donating his talent to the charity fundraiser.

THE RING

Once there was a woman who was very religious and very moral. She was always aware of the fact that life involves constantly choosing right over wrong.

In recognition of her dedication the leader of her church gave her a special gold ring to wear on her finger.

After a time the woman noticed that she had been looking at the hands of other people in the church to see which of them had similar rings.

When she saw people without a ring she could not help but feel superior to them.

Knowing that it was wrong that she should feel this way, she wandered the streets of her town wondering what to do. She began to wish she had never received the ring.

Then she came across a woman about the same age as herself holding out a cup, begging for coins. Having first made sure that the woman did not belong to a church, she put the ring into the cup.

When the other woman started to thank her she said: "No, thank you. You have relieved me of my burden."

part seven

wonder

THE LAW

Once there was a group of archaeologists who were studying the remains of a civilization which had disappeared centuries earlier. They wanted to know why it had not survived.

What was most mysterious was that there had been an overabundance of luxury items and yet there was an insufficient supply of the items needed to meet basic human needs.

While searching through some books preserved under the rubble of an ancient school library, they found a text book on economics which explained everything.

It seemed that the people had believed religiously in what they had called "The Law of Supply and Demand". According to the textbook, to break this Law Of Nature would be to risk terrible unknown consequences.

According to this Law, measuring the amount of money available to buy a certain thing was the only correct method of determining the amount of need for it.

The textbook was full of equations with 'Demand' on one side and 'Supply' on the other.

It was written that if certain people had no money at all, then their demand for goods would be zero. It was clear that to avoid breaking the eternal laws of economics, mathematics and nature, the supply of goods to those people must also be zero.

The archaeologists had made a rare find indeed.

THE JOURNEY

Once there was a young boy whose father invited him to go on a journey. The father wanted to teach the boy about life by letting him experience many different cultures.

The boy noticed that wherever they went his father wanted to know whether the people believed in a higher power or a God of any sort.

The boy also noticed that the gods people talked about sounded a lot like the God his father had told him about, but had very strange sounding names.

After each visit the father would remind the boy that these were not the same as the true, real God of their own religion.

At first the boy answered eagerly: "Yes father. That is just what I was thinking too."

As the pair continued on their journey the boy's response to his father's reminder was less and less confident.

Then one day when their journey was almost finished and they were walking along a quiet road, the young boy looked up and asked: "Father, if I were to change my name, would you still know me?"

THE LEAVES

Once there were four young deer who lived in a wooded spot near a large city. They were very curious about how humans lived and what they ate but they were afraid to go into the city.

Then one day the deer discovered that if they ate the leaves of a certain rare weed they would become invisible to humans.

Feeling confident now, they stepped quietly through the streets of the city unseen. Two of them watched how the people acted on the streets and the other two looked into the windows of the peoples' homes.

When the four deer returned to the woods they discussed what they had observed.

They found it particularly interesting that the humans treated their food very differently depending upon where they were at the time.

When the people were in their homes they fussed over their food — cutting, mixing, heating and arranging everything perfectly before eating it.

But when they were outside on the street they just ate whatever it was that they kept in the large round containers behind the buildings.

THE LEGALITY

Once there was a man who was facing a simple dilemma.

He had been informed that by the authority of an obscure law he was entitled to claim ownership of a portion of his neighbour's property.

Doubting that this could be true he consulted several lawyers who all explained that this was indeed the case.

Not knowing what he should do with this information he consulted family members, friends and even clergy.

Some said that willfully taking advantage would be immoral. Some said that if he did not exercise his legal rights he would be weakening the structure of society.

Then someone asked him a question that he had heard before but had never known how to answer. That question was: "Are you your brother's keeper?"

This time the answer came to him and he said: "Your question answers itself. I am my brother's brother."

The story of the man's dilemma and his answer made its way around town and the law was quietly struck down.

THE PARTICLE

Once there was a little girl whose father was a scientist. The girl loved to ask her father questions about the world and her father loved to answer them. Sometimes he had to tell her that he didn't know the answer and sometimes he even had to tell her that no one knew the answer. This made her all the more curious and it made her want to ask the most difficult questions.

When the girl grew up she became a scientist like her father. One of her goals was to try to find the smallest particle of matter in the universe. Her father began asking her questions about her work, and he tried to find questions that were unanswerable.

The girl gladly shared all the latest discoveries with her father and told him that she was confident that in time science would discover all that there was to know about the universe. It was simply a question of finding the smallest particle and studying its behavior.

One day after she had said this yet again, the father asked her: "Where will you keep all of this knowledge?"

She answered: "Well, in books and on computer files of course."

"No that is not the knowledge I am asking about." the father replied. "Where will you keep the awareness of this knowledge, in other words the knowledge that you have learned all that there is to learn?"

"In my brain of course." she replied. "You mean in your head which is made of the smallest particles in the

Universe?" continued the father. "Yes of course" she replied again, becoming a little tired of the subject and not being used to such persistent questioning.

"So when you do find the smallest particle that everything is made of, including your brain, will that particle already be conscious? Will it know that it has been found? Or is your consciousness just the result of a certain way of combining identical unconscious particles?"

The woman turned to her father and asked: "How did you ever put up with all of my questions when I was growing up?"

THE MIRACLE

Once there was a young cello player who watched as a preacher touched sick people one by one on the forehead and said a few words. One by one the people fell backwards into the arms of a waiting attendant and then claimed to be free of their previous ailment.

The musician knew that the preacher did not have healing powers and she could not understand how people could believe in him. They must have been a bit crazy.

Many years later the cellist developed a painful muscle condition in her wrist which was making it almost impossible for her to perform.

Her whole life was music and not playing was inconceivable. To give up music would be to give up life itself. It was just not imaginable. She became angry and desperate at the same time.

Suddenly and without reason these feelings transformed themselves into an absolute and inexplicable confidence.

Then the musician demanded that the muscles heal themselves. The muscles must do this and would do this. There could be no other possible outcome.

The wrist began to get warm and in a matter of minutes the pain was gone. The young cellist was only mildly surprised since she had been so perfectly confident.

She never told anyone this story because she knew that they would think she was a bit crazy.

THE HERON

Once there was a heron who lived a solitary life in a very shallow pond near a roadway.

Each day the heron went about his business stepping carefully from stone to log to sandy spot finding interesting and edible things along the way.

And each day he would watch the cars and trucks speeding by on the dusty road, wondering how and why they moved so quickly.

The drivers would look over at him and many of them wondered what the beautiful creature might be thinking about them.

They knew that the heron must see their cars and wonder at their speed.

But what they didn't know was that the heron never wondered where they were going.

The heron knew something that the drivers didn't.

There was nowhere to go.

notes & quotes

NOTES

The quotes on the opposite page are from a book called <u>The Blood People, A Division of the Blackfoot Confederacy</u>, by Adolph Hungry Wolf.

In this unique book, Mr. Hungry Wolf describes the struggle of his people to preserve the practice and the meaning of the old traditions.

These particular passages have to do with the introduction of money into their society.

The second of the two quotes relates to a specific incident during which the most sacred of possessions is being exchanged.

"Outside influences came to displace this idea of exchange, trading one item for another, and replacing it with the concept of "payment". It wasn't long before most of our People began to apply this payment philosophy to our Old Ways. Some began to regard the sacrifice of exchanging material things for holy things as a form of payment. As the Old Ways eroded, and the spiritual meaning of things like these exchanges became lost, it gradually became fact that our People bought their sacred Bundles by "paying" for them. Some of our people even began to believe that such Power could be bought and sold...."[1]

"...So we offered a thoroughbred quarter horse and a good mare with a colt. Instead of the other four horses, we offered a large number of twenty-dollar bills sewn to a Hudson's Bay blanket, according to custom, and also a large pile of blankets, clothes, and dry goods."[2]

---

[1] Hungry Wolf: The Blood People, p 80
[2] Hungry Wolf: The Blood People, p 140

In his book <u>The Trouble with Physics</u>, scientist and author Dr. Lee Smolin provides the layman with a wonderful overview of the progress of science.

In the first quote on the opposite page, Dr. Smolin is discussing how mathematics can be used to formulate theories which attempt to explain our physical reality.

If I understand him correctly however, part of what he is saying is that there have been some theories which, while mathematically correct, did not correspond with reality.

The second quote describes what happened to some mathematical physicists when their string theories lacked demonstrable connections to real situations.

This passage was written a couple of years or so before the latest world financial crisis, which some have alleged was caused at least in part by an over-reliance on mathematical algorithms.

Of course, the fact that some brilliant mathematicians left physics and went into banking is not proof of any cause-and-effect relationship. It is not proof that bankers used mathematical formulae that did not correspond with reality, thus causing the mortgage markets to crash. This is admittedly pure speculation.

So it may be unfair for me to include this second quote here. But after all, if there is one thing that our bankers and stock market folks shouldn't mind, it's a little friendly speculation, whether based upon mathematics or not.

"There was no complete formulation of string theory. All we had was a list of hundreds of thousands of distinct theories, each with many free constants. We had no precise idea which of the many versions of the theory corresponded to reality."[3]

"Luckily, working on string theory had proved to be good intellectual training, and some former string theorists are now flourishing in other areas, such as solid-state physics, biology, neuroscience, computers, and banking."[4]

---

[3] Lee Smolin: The Trouble with Physics, p 128
[4] Lee Smolin: The Trouble with Physics, p 128

NOTES

The next quote (opposite) comes from a guy who had experience with making and spending millions of dollars.

I always liked what Ross Perot said about what happens when you spend a million dollars.

The inference I take from this quote is that when someone tells you how much something costs, it is okay to ask why.

Ross Perot was a businessman who ran for President of the U.S. in 1992 and 1996.

QUOTE

"Every time you spend a million dollars, somebody's gettin' it."[5]

---

[5] Ross Perot during his 1996 Presidential Campaign.

NOTES

Our last quote on the opposite page comes from an expert who puts the whole discussion of problems and solutions into perspective.

Sometimes by looking for too many solutions we can lose sight of the problems that really matter.

If we bought all the plant remedies at the garden supply we might not have room for a garden.

"When you start to discover all the things that can go wrong in the garden, it's easy to imagine that every spot, mark, fallen leaf, misshapen growth, or creepy crawly is sinister. Thankfully, this is not the case, and what you see may be a natural part of the plant's cycle of growth, a pest or disease of little consequence to a healthy plant, or simply part of the fascinating diversity of life in the garden."[6]

---

[6] Jo Whittingham: Garden Rescue, p 32

BIBLIOGRAPHY

Hungry Wolf, Adolph: The Blood People;
   A Division of   the Blackfoot Confederacy.
   Harper & Row, New York, 1977

Smolin, Lee PhD: The Trouble With Physics:
   Houghton Mifflin Co., Boston, 2006

Whittingham, Jo: Garden Rescue;
   First aid for plants and flowers. DK Publishing,
   New York 2013